FREEDOM SUMMER

Celebrating the 50th Anniversary of the Freedom Summer

written by **Deborah Wiles**

illustrated by **Jerome Lagarrigue**

ATHENEUM BOOKS FOR YOUNG READERS

New York London Toronto Sydney New Delhi

For the children of the Movement
—D. W.

atheneum

ATHENEUM BOOKS FOR YOUNG READERS

An imprint of Simon & Schuster Children's Publishing Division

1230 Avenue of the Americas, New York, New York 10020

Text copyright © 2001 by Deborah Wiles

Illustrations copyright © 2001 by Jerome Lagarrigue

Foreword copyright © 2014 by Deborah Wiles

For information about special discounts for bulk purchases, please contact Simon & Schuster Special Sales at 1-866-506-1949

or business@simonandschuster.com.

The Simon & Schuster Speakers Bureau can bring authors to your live event. For more information or to book an event, contact

the Simon & Schuster Speakers Bureau at 1-866-248-3049 or visit our website at www.simonspeakers.com.

Book design by Ann Bobco

The text for this book is set in Centaur MT.

The illustrations for this book are rendered in acrylic on paper.

Manufactured in China

0314 SCP

10 9 8 7 6 5 4 3 2 1

CIP data for this book is available from the Library of Congress.

ISBN 978-1-4814-2298-7

Acknowledgments:

I'm grateful for Anne Schwartz's sensibilities and Caitlin Van Dusen's assistance; for Deborah Hopkinson's question, "What story do you really want to tell?"; for the support of my family, my fellow writers and the Minis; and for the talents of Jerome Lagarrigue, the enthusiasm of my librarian friends at the C. Burr Artz library in Frederick, Maryland, and special contributions of James Walker, Chrystal Jeter, and Fredrick and Patricia McKissack.   —D. W.

FOREWORD TO THE ANNIVERSARY EDITION

Fifty years ago, one thousand American college students from the north and west—most from ivy league schools and families with means, and most of them white—came to Mississippi to register African-American citizens to vote. They were called "invaders" by white Mississippians. Black Mississippians called them "freedom workers" or "civil righters." They called themselves "summer volunteers." These young people, and the black citizens they recruited to the cause, changed the political landscape of Mississippi—and subsequently the United States—in the summer of 1964, a summer that became known as "Freedom Summer."

During Freedom Summer, a civil rights act was passed by the federal government that declared, among other things, that all Americans had the right to enjoy public places, no matter their skin color. Many white-owned businesses in the South—including restaurants, swimming pools, and public libraries—closed or became private clubs. The South was determined to keep the races segregated. They were separate, but not equal.

African-Americans had been freed from slavery by the Emancipation Proclamation in 1863 and by the passage of the Thirteenth Amendment to the US Constitution in 1865. As the Southern states rejoined the Union after the Civil War, the Thirteenth, Fourteenth, and Fifteenth Amendments—the Reconstruction Amendments—were passed to protect newly freed black citizens and give them the same rights and privileges as their white counterparts, which included the right to vote. Black citizens voted for the first time in 1867, and some owned property as well.

Southern states, including Mississippi, wanted no part of Reconstruction. They declared that "states' rights" were to be obeyed before any federal mandate and began to pass Jim Crow laws that set African-Americans back to where they had been during the long years of slavery: without protection, without rights, and without the vote to change these laws.

The modern civil rights movement grew as a response to Jim Crow and other discriminatory practices throughout the United States. The Student Non-Violent Coordinating Committee, or SNCC as it came to be known, was formed by Ella Baker in 1960 to harness the energy of young people who wanted to make a difference and to fight segregation. A mock

"Freedom Vote," conducted by SNCC in 1963, was so successful that SNCC believed blacks would turn out in great numbers to vote in the 1964 presidential election—if they had the chance.

In 1964, 45 percent of Mississippi's population was black, but only 5 percent of blacks were registered to vote. Loss of jobs, arrests, and beatings were just some of the very real reprisals African-Americans endured if they tried to register to vote, so most did not even try.

The architects of Freedom Summer were the SNCC, the NAACP (National Association for the Advancement of Colored People), CORE (Congress of Racial Equality), and the SCLC (Southern Christian Leadership Conference). In the summer of 1964, they called themselves COFO, the Council of Federated Organizations, and they recruited students, ministers, doctors, and lawyers to come to Mississippi. They counted on the national press to notice them. And they did.

Volunteers were beaten and arrested over and over again as they opened community centers for black citizens to gather in, started Freedom Schools to teach black children their history, and took black citizens to the courthouse to try and register to vote. Three were killed. Thirty-seven churches were bombed. Thirty homes and businesses were destroyed.

The Mississippi Freedom Democratic Party, organized by Freedom Summer volunteers as an alternative to the all-white Democratic Party, registered more than eighty thousand black voters and took a delegation to the Democratic National Convention in 1964, where they asked to be seated. They were not. But they had proven that African-Americans did want the vote. Their actions had a direct effect on the passage of the Voting Rights Act of 1965.

Fifty years later, the right to vote is still a crucial and fundamental tool of democracy. In 2014, 28 percent of Mississippi's elected state legislature is black, and there are scores of black mayors, police officers, and county officials across the state. The United States has made great strides toward civil rights for every American. There is still much work to be done.

Fannie Lou Hamer, a life-long resident of Mississippi, tireless civil rights activist, and Freedom Summer volunteer perhaps said it best: "Nobody's free until everybody's free."

—D. W.

A NOTE ABOUT THE TEXT

In the early 1960s the American South had long been a place where black Americans could not drink from the same drinking fountains as whites, attend the same schools, or enjoy the same public areas. Then the Civil Rights Act of 1964 became law and stated that "All persons shall be entitled to the full and equal enjoyment" of any public place, regardless of ". . . race, color, religion, or national origin."

I was born a white child in Mobile, Alabama, and spent summers visiting my beloved Mississippi relatives. When the Civil Rights Act was passed, the town pool closed. So did the roller rink and the ice-cream parlor. Rather than lawfully giving blacks the same rights and freedoms as whites, many southern businesses chose to shut their doors in protest. Some of them closed forever.

Also in the summer of 1964, civil rights workers in Mississippi organized "Freedom Summer," a movement to register black Americans to vote. It was a time of great racial violence and change. That was the summer I began to pay attention: I noticed that black Americans used back doors, were often waited on only after every white had been helped, and were often treated poorly, all because of the color of their skin . . . and no matter what any law said. I realized that a white person openly having a black friend, and vice versa, could be a dangerous thing. I couldn't get these thoughts and images out of my mind, and I wondered what it must be like to be a black child my age. I didn't understand these things, and I wondered what any child—black or white—could do to change them. I thought a lot about fairness.

This story grew out of my feelings surrounding that time. It is fiction, but based on real events.

—D. W.

John Henry Waddell is my best friend.

His mama works for my mama.

Her name is Annie Mae.

Every morning at eight o'clock Annie Mae

steps off the county bus

and walks up the long hill to my house.

If it's summer, John Henry is step-step-stepping-it

right beside her.

We like to help Annie Mae.

We shell butter beans. We sweep the front porch.

We let the cats in, then chase the cats out of the house

until Annie Mae says,

"Shoo! Enough of you two! Go play!"

We shoot marbles in the dirt

until we're too hot to be alive.

Then we yell, "Last one in is a rotten egg!"

and run straight for Fiddler's Creek.

John Henry swims better than anybody I know.

He crawls like a catfish, blows bubbles like a swamp monster,

but he doesn't swim in the town pool with me.

He's not allowed.

So we dam the creek with rocks and sticks

to make a swimming spot,

then holler and jump in, wearing only our skin.

John Henry's skin is the color of
browned butter.
He smells like pine needles after a
good rain.
My skin is the color of the pale
moths that dance around the porch
light at night.
John Henry says I smell like a
just-washed sock.
"This means war!" I shout.
We churn that water into a
white hurricane and laugh until
our sides hurt.
Then we float on our backs and
spout like whales.
"I'm gonna be a fireman
when I grow up," I say.
"Me, too," says John Henry.

I have two nickels for ice pops,

so we put on our clothes and walk to town.

John Henry doesn't come with me through the front door

of Mr. Mason's General Store.

He's not allowed.

"How you doin', Young Joe?" asks Mr. Mason. He winks and says,

"You gonna eat these all by yourself?"

My heart does a quick-beat.

"I got one for a friend," I say, and scoot out the door.

"Yessir, it's mighty hot out there!" Mr. Mason calls after me.

"I love ice pops," says John Henry.

"Me, too," I say.

Annie Mae makes dinner for my family every night.

She creams the corn and rolls the biscuits.

Daddy stirs his iced tea and says, "The town pool opens tomorrow

to everybody under the sun, no matter what color."

"That's the new law," Mama tells me.

She helps my plate with peas and says, "It's the way it's going to be now—

Everybody Together—

lunch counters, rest rooms, drinking fountains, too."

I wiggle in my chair like a doodlebug.

"I got to be excused!" I shout, and I run into the kitchen

to tell John Henry.

"I'm gonna swim in the town pool!" he hollers. "Is it deep?"

"REAL deep," I tell him. "And the water's so clear,

 you can jump to the bottom and open your eyes and still see."

"Let's be the first ones there," says John Henry.

"I'll bring my good-luck nickel, and we can dive for it."

Next morning, as soon as the sun peeks into the sky,
here comes my best friend, John Henry Waddell,
run-run-running to meet me.
"Let's go!" he yells, "I got my nickel,"
and I run right with him,
all the way to the town swimming pool.
We race each other over the last hill and . . .
we stop.

County dump trucks are here.

They grind and back up to the empty pool.

Workers rake steaming asphalt into the hole where

sparkling clean water used to be.

One of them is John Henry's big brother, Will Rogers.

We start to call to him, "What happened?"

but he sees us first and points back on down the road—

it means "Git on home!"

But our feet feel stuck, we can't budge.

So we hunker in the tall weeds and watch all morning

until the pool is filled with hot, spongy tar.

Sssssss! Smoky steam rises in the air.

Workers tie planks to their shoes and stomp on the blacktop

to make it smooth.

Will Rogers heaves his shovel into the back of an empty truck

and climbs up with the other workers.

His face is like a storm cloud, and

I know this job has made him angry.

"Let's go!" a boss man shouts, and

the trucks rumble-slam down the road.

It's so quiet now, we can hear the breeze
whisper through the grass.
We sit on the diving board
and stare at the tops of the silver ladders
sticking up from the tar.
My heart beats hard in my chest.
John Henry's voice shakes.
"White folks don't want colored folks
in their pool."
"You're wrong, John Henry," I say,
but I know he's right.
"Let's go back to Fiddler's Creek," I say.
"I didn't want to swim in this old pool
anyway."

John Henry's eyes fill up with angry tears.

"I did," he says. "I wanted to swim in this pool.

I want to do everything you can do."

I don't know what to say,

but as we walk back to town,

my head starts to pop with new ideas.

I want to go to the Dairy Dip with John Henry,

sit down, and share root beer floats.

I want us to go to the picture show, buy popcorn,

and watch the movie together.

I want to see this town with John Henry's eyes.

We stop in front of Mr. Mason's store.

I jam my hands into my pockets

while my mind searches for words to put with my new ideas.

My fingers close around two nickels.

"Want to get an ice pop?"

John Henry wipes his eyes and takes a breath.

"I want to pick it out myself."

I swallow hard and my heart says yes.

"Let's do that," I say.

I give John Henry one of my nickels.

He shakes his head. "I got my own."

We look at each other.

Then we walk through the front door together.